Lineberger Memorial
Library

Lenoir Rhyne University
Lutheran Theological
Southern Seminary
4201 North Main Street, Columbia, SC 29203

DANISH ARTS FOUNDATION

Enchanted Lion Books gratefully acknowledges
the Danish Arts Foundation for its support
towards the translation and production of this book.

Translated from the Danish by Robert Moulthrop

enchantedlionbooks.com

First American edition published in 2016 by Enchanted Lion Books,
351 Van Brunt Street, Brooklyn, NY 11231
Copyright © 2001 by Glenn Ringtved for the text
Copyright © 2001 by Charlotte Pardi for the illustrations
Copyright © 2016 by Robert Moulthrop for the English-language text
Originally published in Denmark in 2001 as *Græd blot hjerte*
All rights reserved under International and Pan-American Copyright Conventions
A CIP record is on file with the Library of Congress
ISBN 978-1-59270-187-2
Printed in China by RR Donnelley Asia Printing Solutions Ltd.

10 9 8 7 6 5 4 3 2 1

Cry, Heart, But Never Break

Glenn Ringtved
Illustrations by Charlotte Pardi

ENCHANTED LION BOOKS
NEW YORK

In the far north, in a small snug house,
four children lived with their beloved grandmother.
A kindly woman, she had cared for them for many years.

Now she had a visitor.

Not wishing to frighten the children,
the visitor had left his scythe outside the door.
All the same, they knew that it was Death.

Nels, the oldest, and his sister, Sonia,
closed their eyes, heavy with sorrow.
Kasper, who was younger, tried to ignore the visitor.
But Leah, the youngest, who was always
getting into trouble, stared straight at Death.

In the quiet, the children could hear their grandmother upstairs, breathing with the same raspy breaths as the figure at the table. They knew Death had come for her and that time was short.

Since everyone knows Death's only friend is night, the children quickly made a plan. They would keep Death away from their grandmother by giving him coffee all through the night. At dawn, he would have no choice but to leave without her.

So every time Death emptied his cup,
Nels would ask, "More coffee, Sir?"
And Death would nod.
Death loved his coffee strong and black like the night,
and he was happy to sit and rest for a while.

Time passed.

Finally, Death was ready. He placed his bony hand over his cup to signal "no more." Then Leah, who had been watching Death all night, reached out and took his hand.

"Oh, Death," she said, "our grandmother is so dear to us, why does she have to die?"

Some people say Death's heart is as dead and black as a piece of coal, but that is not true. Beneath his inky cloak, Death's heart is as red as the most beautiful sunset and beats with a great love of life.

Death wanted to help the children understand, so he said,
"I would like to tell you a story."
And in a strong, sweet voice, he began to speak.
"Once upon a time, so long ago that only I can remember,
there lived two brothers. One was called Sorrow, the other Grief.
Woeful and sad, they moved up and down their gloomy valley.
They went slowly and heavily, and because they never looked up,
they never saw through the shadows to the tops of the hills."

"At the top of those hills, there lived two sisters, Joy and Delight. They were bright and sunny and their days were full of happiness. The only shadow was their sense that something was missing. They didn't know what, but they felt they couldn't fully enjoy their happiness."

Death saw Leah nodding and said,
"I think you can guess what happened next."

"One day the brothers and the sisters met. Sorrow fell instantly in love with Delight, and she with him. It was the same for Grief and Joy. Each couldn't live without the other."

"After their double wedding and a great celebration, the two couples moved into neighboring houses halfway-up and halfway-down the hill. This way the distance to their old homes was the same."

"They all lived to be very old. When the time came to die, Grief and Joy did so on the same day, as did Sorrow and Delight. Their happiness together had been so great that they couldn't live without each other."

"That's a good story," said Nels.

"It is the same with life and death," Death said. "What would life be worth if there were no death? Who would enjoy the sun if it never rained? Who would yearn for day if there were no night?"

The children weren't sure they had understood Death fully, but somehow they knew that he was right.

At last, Death stood up. It was time to go upstairs.
A line of pale gray was edging away the night.

Kasper wanted to stop Death, but Nels held him back.
"No," Nels said. "Life is moving on. This is how it must be."

Moments later, the children heard the upstairs window open.
Then, in a voice somewhere between a cry and a whisper,
Death said, "Fly, Soul. Fly, fly away."

The children hurried upstairs.
They tiptoed into their grandmother's room.
Grandmother had died.

The curtains were blowing in the gentle morning breeze.
Looking at the children, Death said quietly,
"Cry, Heart, but never break. Let your tears of grief
and sadness help begin new life."

Then he was gone.

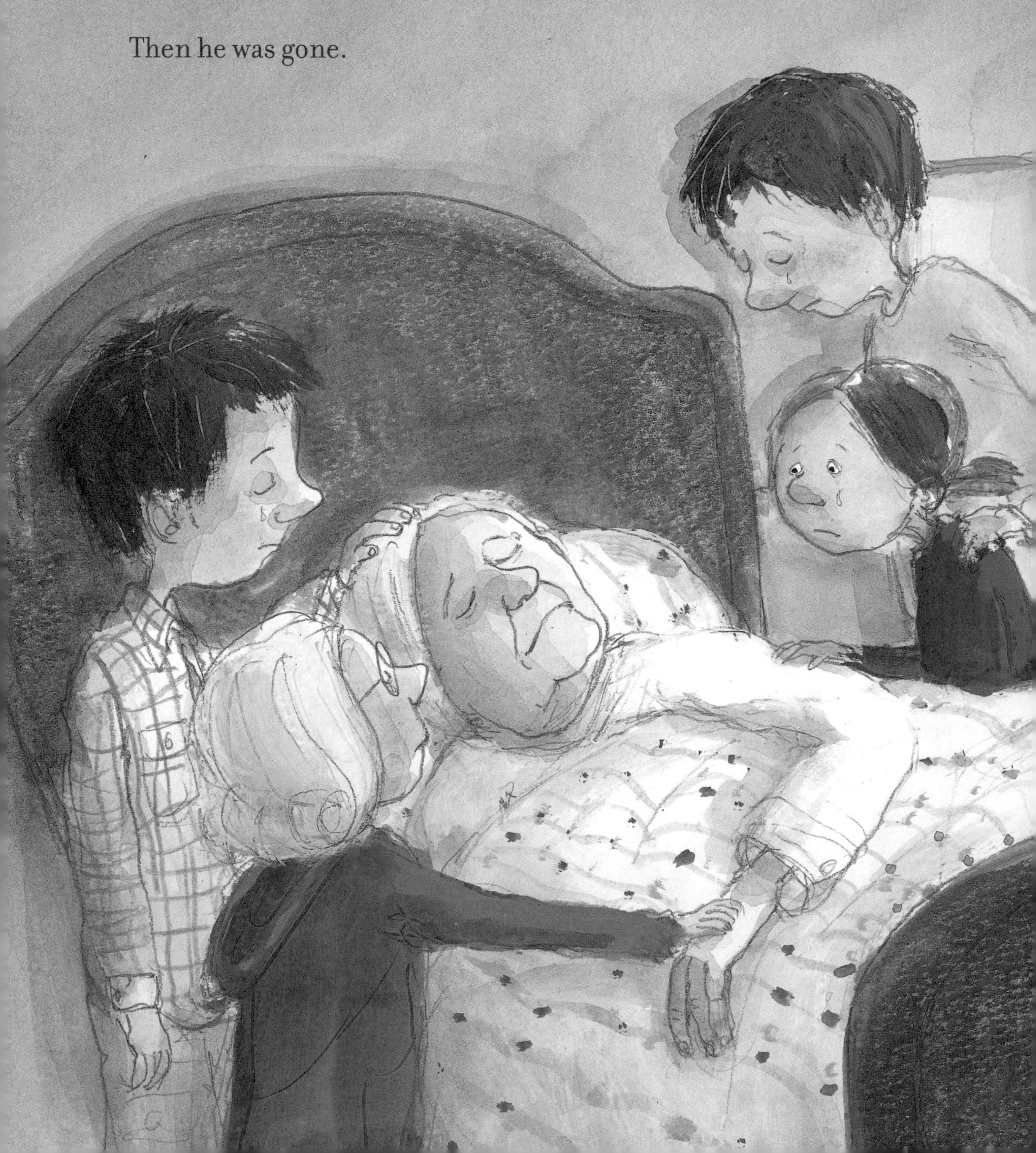

Ever after, whenever the children opened a window, they would think of their grandmother. And when the breeze caressed their faces, they could feel her touch.

In the years that followed, the children lived with their joy and their sorrow, but they always remembered Death's words and took great comfort from their hearts, which grieved and cried but never broke.

LUTHERAN THEOLOGICAL SOUTHERN SEMINARY
3 5898 00166 3414